THIS WALKER BOOK BELONGS TO:

*In memory of
my father*

First published 1993 by Walker Books Ltd
87 Vauxhall Walk, London SE11 5HJ

This edition published 1995

4 6 8 10 9 7 5

© 1993 Kim Lewis

This book has been typeset in Sabon.

Printed in Hong Kong

British Library Cataloguing in Publication Data
A catalogue record for this book
is available from the British Library.

ISBN 0-7445-4325-8

First Snow

KIM LEWIS

WALKER BOOKS
AND SUBSIDIARIES
LONDON • BOSTON • SYDNEY

"Wake up, Sara," whispered Mummy. "Daddy's not very well today. I'm going to feed the sheep on the hill. Would you and Teddy like to come?"

Outside the dogs
were ready and waiting,
bright-eyed and eager to go.
Frost nipped the air. It was
early winter and the rooks
were calling. A wind was
starting to blow.

Through the gate and
up the steep track,
Mummy and Sara climbed.
The sky turned greyer and
the air grew colder.
The dogs raced on ahead.
As they climbed higher,
Sara looked back.
The farmhouse seemed
very small.

At the top of the hill
stood the lone pine tree,
bent by years of winter
winds. Mummy and Sara
stopped below it to rest.
The air went suddenly still.
"We're on top of the world,"
said Mummy, hugging
Sara. "Just you and me
and Teddy."

Across the valley the sky turned white.

Snowflakes lightly danced in the air.

"Look, look!" laughed Sara.

She watched as a snowflake fell on her mitten.

"We'd better feed the sheep," smiled Mummy,

"before it snows too hard."

Sara helped Mummy spread hay on the ground. The sheep were hungry and pushed all around them. Sara tried catching the snow in her hands, but the wind swirled the snowflakes in front of her eyes.

Then the snow fell faster
and stung Sara's cheeks.
The air grew thick and white.
"Come on," said Mummy,
her hand out to Sara.
"The sheep are all right and
we must go home before
the snow gets too deep."

The dogs disappeared through the flying snow.

Snow blotted out the lone pine.

Mummy and Sara started down the track,

hugging close to the wall.

Then suddenly Sara stopped.

"Oh no, where's Teddy?" she cried.

Mummy looked back.
Behind them the snow
was filling their tracks.
"We can't look for Teddy
now," said Mummy.
She whistled for the dogs
and started to walk, but
Sara sat still in the snow.

Then out of the whiteness,
one of the dogs appeared.
She was gently carrying Teddy.
"Oh, Teddy," cried Sara,
hugging him tight.
Mummy picked Sara and
Teddy up.
"Now we can all go home,"
she said.

As they came down the hill, the air cleared
of snow. The sky began turning blue.
Sara and Mummy could see the farmhouse
again, standing snug in the yard.
The world all around them was white and still.

Sara and Mummy
warmed up by the fire.
Then they took Daddy
his breakfast in bed.
"Who's fed the sheep?"
Daddy asked them.
Sara snuggled up
beside him.
"Mummy and Teddy
and me!" she said.

MORE WALKER PAPERBACKS
For You to Enjoy

Also by Kim Lewis

THE SHEPHERD BOY
Shortlisted for the 1991 Kate Greenaway Medal

Through the changing seasons, James watches his farmer father at work
and cannot wait for the day when he can be a farmer too.

"Illustrations that make you want to stroke the page, and a story of such
family warmth and country charm you're left with a warm glow."
Books for Keeps

0-7445-1762-1   £4.99

EMMA'S LAMB
When Emma's dad brings a small lamb into the house
at lambing time, Emma tries to look after it.

"Unsentimental and with wonderfully detailed pictures ... special."
Valerie Bierman, The Scotsman

0-7445-2031-2   £4.99

FLOSS
Floss loves playing ball with the children, but will he make a good sheepdog?

"Kim Lewis draws the English countryside and farm animals as well as any children's illustrator...
A story of warmth and charm ... with a satisfactorily happy ending." *Susan Hill, The Sunday Times*

0-7445-2071-1   £4.99

Walker Paperbacks are available from most booksellers, or by post from B.B.C.S., P.O. Box 941, Hull, North Humberside HU1 3YQ

24 hour telephone credit card line 01482 224626

To order, send: Title, author, ISBN number and price for each book ordered, your full name and address,
cheque or postal order payable to BBCS for the total amount and allow the following for postage and packing:
UK and BFPO: £1.00 for the first book, and 50p for each additional book to a maximum of £3.50.
Overseas and Eire: £2.00 for the first book, £1.00 for the second and 50p for each additional book.

Prices and availability are subject to change without notice.